D M

PUFFIN BOOKS

Sheltie: The Big Show

Make friends with

Sheltie

The little pony with the big heart

Sheltie is the lovable little Shetland pony with a big personality. His best friend and owner is Emma, and together they have lots of exciting adventures.

Share Sheltie and Emma's adventures in

Peter Clover was born and went to school in London. He was a storyboard artist and illustrator before he began to put words to his pictures. He enjoys painting, travelling, cooking and keeping fit, and lives on the coast in Somerset.

Also by Peter Clover in Puffin

The Sheltie series

Sheltie
The Big Show

Peter Clover

PUFFIN BOOKS

Special thanks to Ann Ruffell
To Pieter, Kate and Selina

PUFFIN BOOKS

Published by the Penguin Group
Penguin Books Ltd, 27 Wrights Lane, London W8 5TZ, England
Penguin Putnam Inc., 375 Hudson Street, New York, New York 10014, USA
Penguin Books Australia Ltd, Ringwood, Victoria, Australia
Penguin Books Canada Ltd, 10 Alcorn Avenue, Toronto, Ontario, Canada M4V 3B2
Penguin Books (NZ) Ltd, Private Bag 102902, NSMC, Auckland, New Zealand

On the World Wide Web: www.penguin.com

Penguin Books Ltd, Registered Offices: Harmondsworth, Middlesex, England

First published 1999
1 3 5 7 9 10 8 6 4 2

Created by Working Partners Ltd, London, W12 7QY

The moral right of the author has been asserted

Set in 14/22 Palatino

Made and printed in England by Clays Ltd, St Ives plc

British Library Cataloguing in Publication Data
A CIP catalogue record for this book is available from the British Library

ISBN 0–141–30474–X

Contents

Fun at the Fête

Chapter One

It was a warm and sunny Saturday
morning, and everything looked freshly
washed after last night's rain. Everything,
that is, except Sheltie, Emma's little
Shetland pony. He was so pleased to see
the sun shining that he had decided to
canter right through the muddiest
ground possible, just for the fun of it.

'You're such a mess, Sheltie!' said
Emma after their ride together with her

best friend, Sally, and her pony, Minnow. The two girls had taken their ponies into Sheltie's paddock, at the end of Emma's garden, to clean them up.

'I hope it's sunny next Saturday for the school fête,' said Sally.

Little Applewood School was a hundred years old, and there were going to be three weekends of festivities to celebrate. Mr Price, the headmaster, would unveil a special plaque on the last day.

'I can't believe we go to a school that's so old!' said Emma. 'Next hoof please, Sheltie.' She was brushing Sheltie's legs to try to get rid of the mud. Sheltie blew a raspberry and lifted his other hoof as she reached for it.

'I'm really looking forward to the fête,

aren't you?' Sally asked, as she combed
Minnow's long white mane.

There was going to be a big tent where
all kinds of stalls would be selling crafts
and home-made cakes and jams. Outside
on the school field there would be games

like throwing horseshoes round a pole and knocking coconuts off stands. The whole village was going to take part in the celebrations. They hoped to make lots of money for the school, as well as for their favourite charities, especially the Redwings Horse Sanctuary.

'Dad's going to help on the Horse Sanctuary stall,' said Emma. 'And he says he'll try to win a coconut for us on the coconut shy if he gets time. Mum's going to take Joshua to help her on the home-made jam stall.'

'My dad's running the "Throw a Horseshoe" game,' said Sally. 'He's been collecting old horseshoes for weeks!'

'Isn't it exciting that our class has to design the logo for the school?' said Emma. She hadn't been sure what a logo was until Miss Jenkins, their class teacher, explained that it was a picture that becomes a sign or symbol for something.

'I don't know how we're going to design a picture which will mean Little Applewood. But it would be great if we could win the prize for the best logo.' Emma finished brushing Sheltie and gave him a big hug. 'We ought to have *your* picture on it, Sheltie,' she said. 'Wouldn't that be a good idea?' Sheltie blew a raspberry at Emma.

'No? I suppose you're right, Sheltie,' laughed Emma. 'Not everyone has ponies at Little Applewood School.'

'What about roses?' said Sally. 'Flowers always make a good design.'

Sheltie shook out his newly-combed mane.

'He doesn't seem to think much of that one, either,' grinned Emma.

Sally frowned. She gave her pony a pat on his hindquarters and loosened his girth strap. 'We'll have to think of something really good. There are going to be banners all over the village, decorated with the winner's Little Applewood logo,' she said.

Emma thought hard. 'What about a rosette to show Little Applewood School is the best?'

This time Sheltie shook his head so hard that his mane nearly brushed Emma in the face! The girls laughed. Sheltie just didn't seem to like any of their ideas.

The little Shetland pony suddenly trotted off into his field shelter. He came out almost immediately with something in his mouth and dropped it at Emma's feet.

'What's this, Sheltie?' she said, picking it up. 'Oh – it's one of your little apples. Have you brought me a present?'

And then she smiled.

'Little apples,' she said excitedly to Sally. 'Of course. Little Applewood! Oh, Sheltie, you're so clever! Our banner can be full of little apples on trees.'

'A little apple wood!' said Sally. 'Emma, you have the cleverest pony in the entire world!'

At school on Monday, Miss Jenkins looked at everyone's ideas. There were pictures of the school and pictures of the village, but none of them seemed quite right for a logo design.

Then Miss Jenkins held up Sally and Emma's picture of the little apple trees.

'This one is very simple, so it would make a good logo. It will be easy to make lots of copies, but the main reason why this one would work best is that it represents the name of our school, Little Applewood. It's so simple. Well done, Emma and Sally.'

'And Sheltie!' whispered Emma. The two friends grinned happily at each other.

Chapter Two

That evening, Emma thought Sheltie
deserved an extra long ride. She held the
reins loosely so that Sheltie could choose
where he wanted to go.

The little pony trotted off with his pale
mane flying and his tail swishing
backwards and forwards. He took Emma
round by Mr Brown's meadow, past
Horseshoe Pond, down the lane that
went by the woods, and along by the big

field at the bottom of the hill. There at the field gate was a big notice on a post, advertising a car boot sale.

'Shall we go to the sale, Sheltie?' asked Emma. 'There might be something interesting to buy.'

She looked more closely. It was on Saturday – exactly the same day as the school fête. Emma was excited – two events in Little Applewood on the same day!

CAR BOOT
SALE
HERE ON
SATURDAY

She quickly rode home to tell her mum and dad about the car boot sale.

Dad was busy mending a bit of fence at the bottom of the garden. He listened as Emma told him about the sale.

'PC Green and PC McDonald will have a busy day,' he said, whacking a post into the ground with a big sledgehammer.

'Why?' asked Emma.

'Because the roads will be crammed full of people driving to the sale. They will need to direct all the traffic. Pity all those people don't know about our fête. We'd get lots more money for the school if they did.'

'I've got an idea,' said Emma suddenly. 'I'm just going to visit Sally. I'll be back soon.'

She turned Sheltie round and rode
through the lanes to Fox Hall Manor,
where Sally lived.

When she got there, Emma told Sally
about the car boot sale sign while the
ponies rubbed noses.

'Dad said there would be lots of people
going to the car boot sale,' said Emma. 'I
thought if we put our own sign up as
well, then we'd get even more people to
come to our fête.'

'What a good idea,' said Sally. 'Let's
make a sign straight away.'

They painted a simple sign in big
bright letters on a sheet of white card.
Then they rode back to Emma's house.
Dad had finished mending the fence,
but there were a few wooden posts left
over.

'Could we use one of those posts to stick our sign on?' she asked.

'Why not?' said Dad. He chose the straightest one and gave it to Sally.

'I think I've got just the thing to fasten the card to,' said Mum. She found an old pinboard in the cupboard. 'We'll pin your sign on to this and then I'll put some plastic over the whole thing so that if it rains, the paint won't run.'

Dad nailed the post on to the pinboard.

The sign looked really good when they had finished. It had their special Little Applewood logo on it too.

Mr Crock, Emma's neighbour, came round to bring them a fresh cabbage from his garden.

'That's a grand sign,' he said. 'Where are you going to put it?'

Emma and Sally explained.

'I'll bet you get lots more people at the fête now,' said Mr Crock.

A few minutes later, Emma's dad drove the car to the field where the car boot sale was going to be. Emma and Sally followed on their ponies.

Dad whacked in the fence post with his

sledgehammer. Then they all stood back a bit to see the sign properly.

'That should do the trick,' said Emma, pleased.

But when Emma rode over to the field the next evening to admire her notice, she had a shock.

Their beautiful new signpost had been pulled up like a weed and thrown to the ground. It was broken in two!

'Who could have done that, Sheltie?' asked Emma, feeling very cross.

'I did!' said a gruff voice.

A man with greasy blond hair and an angry face came striding towards them. He pointed to his car boot sale notice. 'I've rented this field for my sale,' he said. 'You can't put your sign up in the same place. People might go to your silly little fête instead of to my sale.'

'It's not a silly little fête,' said Emma. Sheltie blew noisily down his nostrils with an angry snort. Emma pulled her pony back out of the way. 'It's our school's hundredth anniversary,' she went on. 'We want lots of people to come

and raise money for charity.'

'Then have it on a different day!' snapped the man. 'I got here first. Now go away and take that shaggy monster with you!'

Sheltie didn't like to hear Emma being shouted at like that. He flattened his ears and ground his teeth.

'And if that thing bites me, I'll have the police on to you!'

Then the man strode off across the field to a big car which was parked on the other side.

Chapter Three

After the man had left, Sheltie nosed at
the signpost lying on the grass.

'It's no good, Sheltie,' said Emma sadly.
'It's broken.'

But Sheltie pushed his front hoof at
the board and tipped it over and Emma
saw that the sign wasn't broken after all.
The plastic that Mum had put over their
poster was a bit torn at the edges, but
the board was still in one piece, even

though it had come unstuck from the post.

Emma slid off Sheltie's back, picked up the board and the post and led the little pony home.

'Never mind,' said Dad, when Emma showed him the broken sign. 'I can mend it easily. He hasn't damaged it very much. And I can see the man's point. He doesn't want all his customers suddenly rushing off to spend their money somewhere else.'

'I suppose not,' said Emma, trying to be fair. 'But it would be nice if people could go to both. And he didn't have to be so rude about it. *We* weren't rude to him.'

'Why don't you put the board up on the other side of the village?' said Mum.

'Nobody will mind it being there, and who knows, maybe we'll get lots of people going to both the car boot sale *and* our fête.'

So Dad mended the signpost and together they set it up on the other side of the village, near Fox Hall Manor.

At school everyone was getting ready for the fête. Miss Jenkins showed Emma's class how to make prints from potatoes cut in half. Some of the class cut trunks out of their half-potatoes. Others did round shapes to print the green tops of the trees. The rest of the class made small round shapes for the bright red apples on the trees.

Soon everyone could see how the first banner was going to look.

23

'It will take ages,' whispered Sally to Emma.

'I know,' Emma whispered back. 'But doesn't it look great?'

The banners were finished a couple of days before the fête. Miss Jenkins asked for volunteers with ponies to do the job of hanging them between the trees round the school playing field.

'You'd need to be a giant to reach some of those trees,' she smiled. 'But those of you with ponies will do the job perfectly.'

After school the next day, Emma and Sheltie came along to help hang up the banners. Simon and Melody came too on their ponies, Midnight and Sapphire. They soon started pushing and shoving the other ponies. Simon and Melody

usually caused trouble whenever they
turned up.

'Get out of the way,' Melody told
Emma, as Sapphire barged into Sheltie. 'If
you don't know how to ride, don't try to
help.'

'You'll be no use if Sheltie won't stand
still,' sneered Simon.

Emma was indignant. 'But you got in *our* way!' she said, patting Sheltie's neck in case Sapphire had upset him.

Miss Jenkins stood on the field in her jeans and trainers and told the riders where to go and what to do. Some of the ponies seemed rather excited. Emma thought it was because Simon and Melody were still barging into everyone.

'Midnight first,' called Miss Jenkins' clear voice. Simon kicked Midnight into a trot and went over to the big chestnut tree. 'And now Sapphire,' she called again.

Emma could see what Miss Jenkins was doing. With those two out of the way, the other ponies calmed down.

But Midnight and Sapphire were very naughty. They pranced about so much, it was almost impossible for Simon or Melody to stand in the stirrups with the banners. At last, Miss Jenkins had to hold Midnight while Simon took hold of one end of the banner. He lifted it high to fix it on to a branch of the big tree. Melody was supposed to fix the other end of the banner to another branch, but Sapphire danced around in a circle so that the whole banner twisted in her hands.

'Stupid pony!' shouted Melody. 'I can't do it now!' She dropped her end of the banner and let Sapphire canter off to the other side of the field.

'Dear me,' said Miss Jenkins, raising her eyebrows. 'Come on, Emma, see if you can fix the other end.'

'You'll behave, won't you, Sheltie?' whispered Emma.

Sheltie snorted. Of course he would! Emma carefully walked Sheltie over to where Miss Jenkins was pointing and stood up in the stirrups.

'Can you reach?' asked Miss Jenkins.

Sheltie wasn't as tall as Sapphire, but he was much less nervous. Emma lifted her arms. She managed to reach one of the lower branches. Sheltie stood very still underneath her. 'Yes,' she said.

Miss Jenkins carried the drooping end of the banner over to Emma who lifted it to the branch and tied it on with the tapes.

'Well done, Emma,' said Miss Jenkins.

Emma slid back on to her saddle and patted her little Shetland pony on the neck. 'Well done, Sheltie,' she said.

Now that the banners were up and the other classes had finished their painted red and green garlands for the stalls, there was only one thing left to do.

On Friday, the whole school was given the afternoon off for a special anniversary

HAPPY 100TH BIRTHDAY LITTLE APPLEWOOD SCHOOL

holiday. But some people were needed to blow up hundreds of red and yellow balloons on the school field. These were going to be hung all over the big tent.

Emma and Sally brought out the big plastic nets to stop the balloons from sailing away when they were blown up.

'What fun, having an afternoon off to blow up balloons,' said Mum. She had brought Emma's little brother, Joshua, along on Sheltie's back to watch.

It sounded like fun, but it was harder work than anybody expected.

'You don't call this an afternoon off, do you?' said Emma. She had already blown up twenty balloons and was feeling a bit dizzy.

'Balloon!' said Joshua, so Emma gave him a red one to play with. Then she

leaned against Sheltie to have a rest
from blowing up balloons. Sheltie
nudged her shoulders and tried to take
one of the little rubber balloons out of
its bag.

'No, Sheltie, you'd eat it and then
you'd be ill,' Emma told him. 'But you
can have a blown-up yellow one to play
with if you like. Here you are.'

She put a blown-up balloon down on
the ground in front of him. Sheltie shook
his mane, snorted and stamped on the
ground with his right hoof.

Unfortunately the balloon was right
underneath his hoof. *Bang!* The balloon
burst. Joshua looked startled and let go of
his balloon.

Sheltie walked over to it and lifted his
hoof again.

'No, Sheltie! You'll frighten Joshua!' scolded Emma.

But Joshua grinned at Sheltie. He clapped his hands. 'Bang!' he cried. Sheltie stepped on the red balloon and popped it. Joshua laughed. So did Mum and Sally.

'Sheltie! You are naughty!' said Emma.
'You don't think I've spent all this time
blowing up balloons just for you to pop
them, do you?'

'I wish Sheltie's mouth was the right
shape for blowing up balloons,' said
Sally. 'That would save us a lot of time.'

Emma ruffled Sheltie's mane. 'You're
the cleverest pony in the world, Sheltie.
But even you couldn't do that.'

When the balloons were all blown up
and put into the nets in the school hall,
everybody went home for tea. Afterwards,
Emma took Sheltie out for a ride.

As she came back past the school,
she saw somebody she recognized, right
outside the gate. It was the man from
the car boot sale. He had something

round and brown tucked under his arm.

The man turned and saw Emma. Then suddenly he scuttled off, jumped into his car, and drove quickly away.

Chapter Four

It was the morning of the fête. Dad looked after Joshua so that Mum could go and get the home-made jam set up on her stall.

Emma had things to do too. It was time for the painted garlands and the balloons to be collected from the school hall and brought over to the big tent. Emma was going to use Sheltie's little fish cart to help carry the balloons across.

The doors of the hall were open as Sheltie trotted up, pulling the little cart. Emma pulled gently on the reins to bring Sheltie to a halt. Then she loosely tethered the little pony to a post and went to collect the balloons.

But when she walked inside the hall, she found Mr Grimley, the caretaker, standing there, looking very upset.

'What's happened?' asked Emma.

Mr Grimley just pointed.

Instead of a colourful pile of red and yellow balloons, there was a small heap of bits of rubber. All the balloons had burst – and it looked as though someone had burst them deliberately! Someone had also thrown water over the painted garlands so that all the paint was streaked and smeared. They were ruined!

'Who would want to spoil our fête?'
asked Emma.

Mr Grimley shook his head sadly.
'There's something else as well,' he said.
'Whoever made all this mess has stolen

the special anniversary plaque from Mr Price's office.'

More people started arriving to carry things over to the tent. Soon there was a crowd outside the school, with everybody all talking at once. Who could have done such a terrible thing? Who would want to steal the school's anniversary plaque?

'I need to think, Sheltie,' whispered Emma.

She led Sheltie and the little cart round the other side of the school so that she could be away from everyone rushing around.

But as they passed the back of the school, Sheltie stopped dead and tossed his mane. He sniffed about in the ground below a small window.

Emma looked up. The window of the

storeroom was open and there were dirty
scrape marks down the wall outside it.
Underneath the window, in the soft

ground, were the prints of a large pair of shoes.

'It looks as if whoever spoiled our decorations and stole the plaque must have got into the school this way,' said Emma. 'And I wonder exactly what that car boot sale man was doing by the school yesterday?'

Sheltie whinnied, as if he was wondering too.

Emma jumped back into the little fish cart. 'Come on, Sheltie,' she said. 'I think we should go home.'

When Emma got back to the cottage, she told Dad about the man she had seen outside the school gate. 'It doesn't prove anything,' said Dad. 'But maybe we should phone the police and tell them about it.'

PC Green listened to what Emma had to say. 'I'll go along to the field and ask him what he was doing,' he said.

Emma decided she would ride across to the field to meet PC Green there, just in case he needed someone to point out the man. She unhitched Sheltie from his cart and put his saddle and bridle on. Then she made her way over to the field.

There were already quite a few people there when Emma reached the field. The car boot sale organizers were busily marking out lanes with rope to show where the cars should be parked that afternoon.

Emma and Sheltie rushed up to PC Green who was scanning the field for a man who fitted Emma's description.

'That's him,' said Emma, pointing to the greasy-haired man.

PC Green got out his notebook and walked over towards him.

'You were seen outside Little Applewood School yesterday afternoon,' said PC Green. 'What were you doing there?'

The greasy-haired man quickly became angry. 'What do you mean? I wasn't anywhere near the school last night. You ask my mates. I was with them.'

PC Green began to ask what time that was, but Sheltie took a different approach. He nosed at the man as if he was trying to get at a carrot in his jacket pocket. The man flapped his hand and tried to move away. Sheltie followed and nosed at the other side of his jacket.

'Get that beast away!' he shouted.
'Officer, that animal tried to bite me last
week! Get the brute off my field!'

The man was making such a noise that
the other organizers came over to see
what was going on and saw Sheltie grab

the back of his jacket with his teeth. The back of the man's jacket was smeared with paint.

'See!' said Emma. 'Red and green paint! Those are the colours of the garlands for our fête. They were so pretty and somebody ruined them by throwing water over them.'

'What a shame!' said one of the organizers indignantly.

'I saw him take down a signpost last week,' said someone else. 'Wasn't that a sign advertising your fête?'

'Yes, it was,' said Emma.

Sheltie blew a raspberry and Emma suddenly remembered about the balloons. 'Whoever it was burst hundreds of balloons that we blew up yesterday and stole our anniversary plaque,' said

Emma. 'And I saw this man near the school yesterday.'

'What a dreadful thing to do!' said a lady in stout brown boots. 'I think we ought to look in his car,' she said.

'It wasn't me!' said the greasy-haired man. 'It was somebody else.'

Then Sheltie nosed right into his pocket and brought out a burst balloon.

'I think we'd better take a look at your car right away,' said PC Green.

Emma and Sheltie followed the crowd over to the other side of the field. PC Green made the man open his car boot.

Inside, on top of a pile of second-hand videos, was the anniversary plaque.

'Someone gave it to me for the car boot sale!' he lied.

PC Green laid a heavy hand on the

man's shoulders. 'I think you'd better come along with me,' he said.

By the time Emma got back with her news, everyone in the village had heard about the disaster. They stopped setting up their stalls for a while to blow up some more balloons, but Emma knew that there wouldn't be enough to decorate the big tent and all of the stalls.

'I could get some paper and paint,' said Emma to her mum. 'Sheltie and I could carry it back easily. If we all helped we could make more garlands.' It would be a shame not to have the stalls decorated. At the moment they looked very bare.

'No, Emma,' said Mum. 'We've got to get things set up now – there really isn't time. Never mind – it's what's on the stalls that matters.'

Emma and Sheltie went back towards the playground to find Sally. 'You've been very clever, Sheltie,' said Emma, 'but there's nothing you can do about this. There's no time left.'

Sheltie nudged her arm.

'What is it?' asked Emma. 'Are you trying to tell me something?

The pony whickered. He stamped his feet a few times and then nudged Emma towards the classroom.

Suddenly Emma realized what Sheltie wanted. 'I've got the answer!' she said, her eyes shining.

Emma ran into the school hall where the teachers were still trying to clear up the mess. 'Can I have lots of paint and paper?' she asked. 'It's an emergency.'

In no time at all she was back at the tent clutching bottles of ready-mixed paint and rolls of paper. Mum did what Emma asked and set out shallow paint trays on the hard ground outside with a layer of nice, thick paint in them. Emma unrolled long sheets of paper near the trays.

'All right, Sheltie. Best foot forward,' said Emma.

Sheltie picked up one of his front hooves and dropped it gently into one of the trays of paint. Then he walked along the paper Emma had spread out for him. With each step he left a print of his own horseshoe.

'Sheltie's saved the day again!' said Mr

Crock. 'Let me have those green ones,
Emma. They'll be just the job to hang in
front of my vegetable stall!'

At two o'clock Mr Price, the headmaster,
opened the fête. Emma led Sheltie into
the back of the big tent to watch. The

horseshoe decorations looked great hanging over every stall so that nobody could see the plain wooden legs of the tables.

The afternoon was a huge success. Mum sold all her pots of jam. Dad knocked over two coconuts at the shy and managed to open the end of one of them to give Emma and Joshua a drink of the delicious coconut milk inside. And when people had finished rummaging about at the car boot sale, they came over to Little Applewood School to buy things at the fête and play at the sideshows.

It had been a wonderful day. Everyone enjoyed themselves and lots of money was raised for the school and the charities. And Sheltie had helped to make it all happen!

Let's Have a Party!

Chapter One

The next event celebrating Little Applewood School's one hundredth birthday was going to be a huge party, to be held in the school hall.

Everyone was making lots of food for the party. As Emma and Sheltie trotted back through the village at the end of their evening ride together, the air was filled with delicious baking smells, wafting out of nearly everyone's door.

'That smells like Mrs Smith's gingerbread biscuits!' said Emma.

Sheltie stopped outside the cottage and licked his lips.

'No, Sheltie,' said Emma firmly. 'You know biscuits aren't good for you. You can have a peppermint treat when you get home, but that's all. Walk on.'

Sheltie blew a loud raspberry as if he didn't agree with Emma, but he walked on and soon they were home.

When Emma opened the gate to Sheltie's paddock, she was surprised to see water everywhere.

'But it hasn't rained for a week!' said Emma. 'Unless there's been a very

strange storm just over your paddock,'
she joked. And then she thought of
something. 'You haven't turned your tap
on, have you, Sheltie?'

The little pony trotted over to the tap
to which a hose was attached so that
Emma could fill Sheltie's drinking
trough. The tap was on and water was
flowing gently out of the other end of the
hose. Sheltie lowered his head and took

the tap in his teeth. Then, with a quick twist of his head, he managed to turn the tap off.

'Sheltie, you are clever!' said Emma. 'But if you keep turning the tap on, you'll have the whole field under water!'

Sheltie shook his mane and jangled his bit.

Emma took off his saddle and bridle, hung them over the fence, and began to brush his thick coat. When she had finished, she gave him a pat on his hindquarters and let him run round the field while she put away his tack.

As she walked back to the house, Mum called out, 'Guess what clever Joshua can do? He's learned how to turn on taps. He climbed up on the stool and filled the kitchen sink!'

Oh, is that who turned on Sheltie's tap? thought Emma.

She told Mum and Dad how the paddock was flooded when she came back from her ride. 'I'll have to say sorry to Sheltie. I thought it was him!'

'We'd better make sure all our taps are turned off very tightly from now on,' said Dad. 'By the way, Emma, how would you like to collect all the food for the party on Saturday morning and deliver it to the school hall? You could carry it in Sheltie's fish cart.'

Emma smiled. 'Sheltie and I would love too,' she said.

'When you go for your ride tomorrow evening, maybe you could pop over and tell everyone what time you'll arrive on Saturday morning to pick up the food,'

said Mum. She laughed. 'And keep an
eye on Sheltie! He smelled my chocolate
brownies this morning. Next thing I
knew, he was trying to get into the
kitchen!'

The next evening, Emma took Sheltie
over the little stone bridge at the end of
the lane and made her way towards
Beacon Hill and Marjorie Wallace's
cottage, nestling at the foot of it.

Emma loosely tied Sheltie's rein to the
big metal ring in the cottage wall. She
could smell Marjorie's special coconut
cake, and through the open window she
could see a tray of little cakes cooling on
the window sill.

She knocked on the red painted door.

'Is it all right if I come at ten on

Saturday morning to collect the cakes?'
asked Emma, when Marjorie opened the
cottage door.

'Of course, Emma. Come in and try
one,' said Marjorie, smiling. 'I need
somebody to tell me how they taste.'

So Emma went in and had one of
Marjorie's little coconut cakes and a fizzy
drink to go with it. They were so busy
talking that they didn't see Sheltie's fuzzy
muzzle slide through the open window

and snaffle one of the cakes put out to cool.

'Come on, Sheltie,' said Emma, when she had finished. 'It's time to move on to the next house.'

With a lovely taste of coconut in her mouth, she remounted Sheltie and trotted back along the lanes to Mrs Marsh's cottage at the end of the village.

'Hello, Emma,' said Mrs Marsh. 'I've just finished making some flapjacks. Would you like to try one?'

'Yes, please,' said Emma.

Mrs Marsh brought out some flapjacks on a plate and offered one to Emma. While they were talking, Mrs Marsh put the plate down. Neither of them saw Sheltie turn his head and neatly snaffle a piece of flapjack from the plate!

As she went through the village, Emma was offered lots of scrumptious cakes and biscuits. And at each stop, Sheltie managed to steal something without being seen. Chocolate cookies, marshmallow squares, cupcakes . . . Sheltie sampled them all!

Back at home, Mum and Joshua met Emma at the gate. 'This little monkey has managed to turn on both the kitchen taps again,' said Mum. 'Did you arrange to collect all the cakes?'

Emma undid Sheltie's girth strap and slid the saddle off his back. 'Yes, and I've tasted them all too!' she said.

Chapter Two

As usual, the next morning, Emma got up early to feed Sheltie before going to school.

But when she arrived at the paddock, Sheltie was not at the gate waiting for his scoop of pony mix. 'Sheltie! Where are you?' called Emma. Sheltie didn't come to her call. Then she saw him. He was in the furthest corner of the paddock.

Emma jumped over the gate and ran across the paddock. The little Shetland pony didn't move when she came near, but just stood there. He was sweating as if he'd been galloping for miles across the downs.

'Sheltie! Are you ill?' she cried anxiously. Sheltie was panting hard.

Emma raced back to the house. 'Mum! Dad! Come quickly. Sheltie's ill!'

Mum came downstairs, carrying Joshua in his pyjamas. 'What's the matter, Emma?'

'Sheltie looks very poorly,' said Emma. 'Can you call the vet?'

Dad came out to look at the little pony. 'Poor Sheltie. He does look rather ill,' he said. 'I'll phone Mr Thorne straight away.'

'Tummy ache!' said Joshua, holding his
own tummy.

'Perhaps,' said Mum. 'Did you feed
him any treats last night, Emma?'

'Only a peppermint, when we came
home,' said Emma. She was nearly crying
and fighting to hold back the tears.
Sheltie looked so sad, standing in the

corner of the paddock. 'But he's had lots of peppermints and they've never made him ill before!'

'Then it's probably something quite different,' said Mum calmly. 'Now go and get some breakfast quickly or you'll be late for school.'

'I don't feel like breakfast,' said Emma sadly.

'You must eat,' said Mum firmly. 'You can't go all day without anything inside you.'

Emma tried to eat some cereal, but it didn't want to go down.

'I'm sure Sheltie will be all right,' said Dad as he left to go to work. 'Mr Thorne will be here soon.'

'Can I wait to see him?' Emma asked Mum.

'I'm sorry, Emma,' said Mum. 'You've got to go to school. Don't worry. Mr Thorne will have called by lunchtime and you'll know what's wrong then.'

'Lunchtime!' cried Emma. 'Poor Sheltie! Why does he have to wait so long?'

'Dad has told the vet about Sheltie's symptoms,' said Mum. 'I'm sure it's not serious. If he thought it was, he would have come sooner.'

'Just me being near Sheltie might help him,' said Emma.

'No,' said Mum firmly. 'And now you'd better run or you'll be late.'

Emma thought about Sheltie all morning at school and didn't really listen in her lessons. As soon as lunchtime arrived she

raced home and saw Mr Thorne's Land
Rover outside. Emma went straight to the
paddock. Mum was there with the vet.
Dad had popped home too.

'What's the matter with Sheltie?' Emma
cried.

Mr Thorne saw that she was very
upset.

'Don't worry,' he told her. 'He'll get
better. But he's got a huge tummy ache
just now. It's called colic. He's eaten a lot
of something that's disagreed with him.
What have you given him to eat? Cream
cakes?'

Mr Thorne was joking, but Emma
suddenly thought about their trip
yesterday. 'We went to tell people what
time I'd collect their cakes and biscuits on
Saturday,' she said. 'Lots of them had just

been baking. I ate far too much, but I told everybody not to give Sheltie anything.'

'Very sensible,' smiled Mr Thorne. 'But you've got a clever pony here. If I'm not mistaken, he's been stealing cakes when you weren't looking!'

Mum smiled and told the vet about Sheltie trying to get into the kitchen to eat her chocolate brownies.

'There you are,' said Mr Thorne. 'I expect that's what's happened. Now I'm going to give him a pain-killing injection. He should be all right again in a few hours.' Sheltie gave a loud belch and lowered his head.

Before going back to school, Emma and Dad went down to the paddock again. 'Poor Sheltie,' whispered Emma.

'Sometimes your eyes are too big for your belly!'

Then she had an awful thought. Next day was the party. How was she going to do her collecting if Sheltie was ill?

'Please get better soon,' she said to him. 'We've got all the cakes to collect!'

Sheltie looked very sorry for himself. Poor greedy little pony!

Chapter Three

Sheltie was still poorly when Emma
arrived home from school.

'Don't worry,' said Mum. 'If he's still
not himself tomorrow, Dad will take you
round to collect the cakes in the car.'

'But Sheltie will miss all the fun,' said
Emma sadly. 'I'm going down to the
paddock to see how he is.'

Sheltie was still looking miserable,
even in his favourite corner of the

paddock. All Emma could do was whisper in his ear and stroke his tangled mane. She didn't try to brush it in case she disturbed him. She stood by his side for quite a long time before going back to the house.

Emma looked so unhappy her mum said, 'Come to the school and help decorate the hall for the party. It'll cheer you up. Dad is coming to help set up tables and chairs.'

Emma smiled weakly. She didn't like feeling so glum and perhaps decorating the hall might make her feel better.

So after tea they all walked down to the hall with Joshua in his pushchair. Even that made Emma sad. 'If Sheltie wasn't ill, he could have given Joshua a ride down to the hall.'

'Sheltie poorly,' said Joshua with a sad face.

'I'm sure he'll be completely better by tomorrow,' said Dad. 'Didn't Mr Thorne say so?'

It seemed as if everybody in the village had heard of Sheltie's tummy ache. As they went past, Mr Crock asked how he was. So did Mrs Marsh.

Emma cheered up a little when they arrived at the school hall. It smelled lovely with heaps of flowers waiting to be arranged in big vases.

'We could stick Sheltie's horseshoe prints round the walls so that everyone can see it's Little Applewood's party day,' said Mum. 'We saved them when we took the stalls down after the fête. Do you know where Mr Grimley put them?'

'They're in our classroom,' said Emma. 'Shall I take Joshua to look for them?'

Mum smiled at Joshua. 'That's a good idea,' she said. 'It will keep him busy while we're arranging the flowers.'

Emma and Joshua found the horseshoe-print banners and Mrs Marsh helped stick them on the walls while Mum and her friends arranged the flowers. Dad and the other helpers put up the tables.

First they had to set up the folding legs, called trestles, in lines. After that they put the table tops, like long planks of wood, on top. There was a lot of clattering and banging as they shifted the trestles about.

'Be careful!' cried Emma. 'Joshua's

under there!' She crawled between the trestles and pulled him out of the way.

'It's too dangerous for Joshua in here,' said Dad. 'Will you take him out of the way please, Emma?'

Emma decided to get Joshua to help stick up pictures, but he soon got bored and went to explore round the little cupboards and rooms at the back of the hall. Then, as soon as all the tables were

up, he decided to play underneath them instead.

'I suppose he can't do any harm there,' said Mum. 'We'll be finished soon, then it will be time for him to go to bed.'

As soon as they got home, Emma went down to the paddock.

Sheltie was standing by the gate, just as if nothing had happened to him! His brown eyes twinkled beneath his long mane. Then he blew a wet raspberry at Emma, as if to say, 'Where's my dinner?'

Emma jumped over the gate and threw her arms round his neck.

'Sheltie, are you really better? You cheeky pony! There'll be nothing but carrots and pony mix for you from now on!'

Sheltie pushed his soft, velvety muzzle

into her pocket. It was just as if he was already looking for a lovely sweet carrot.

On Saturday morning Emma got up early again. She wanted to make Sheltie look really smart before going on their cake-collecting round.

Sheltie was very frisky after his day of

sickness. He didn't care about having his
mane brushed. He stood still long enough
for his tail to be untangled, but he didn't
wait for it to be plaited. The little pony
pranced about by his shelter, shaking his
head.

Emma giggled. He was being naughty,
but she was so pleased that he was better,
she didn't want to scold him.

At last Sheltie calmed down and Emma
was able to put on his saddle and bridle.

Emma went back to tell Mum and Dad
where she was going. Dad was eating
breakfast, still in his pyjamas. He smiled
at Emma. 'Aren't you too early?' he said.
'What time did you say you'd collect
your cakes?'

Joshua waved his toast and honey.
'Sheltie poorly,' he said.

'No, he's all better now!' said Emma. 'I'm taking him for a nice long ride to tire him out before we try harnessing him to the cart. He's so frisky he might go too fast and then all the cakes will fall out.'

'We can't have that,' said Dad. 'What time will you be back? Nine o'clock? I might have got up properly by then,' he joked.

Emma laughed. She didn't know how he could stay in his pyjamas on a lovely bright day like this.

Emma took Sheltie up on the downs so that the little pony could have a good gallop. Sheltie pranced and shook his mane, glad to feel well again and enjoy the sunshine. When they got home, Dad helped her to harness Sheltie to his cart

and then Emma set off for Marjorie
Wallace's cottage at the bottom of Beacon
Hill.

'I hope there will be room for you, as
well as all the food,' laughed Marjorie.
'From what I hear, there will be enough
to feed the whole village for weeks!'

She brought out her coconut cakes in a plastic box and packed them carefully into the bottom of the little cart.

'I saved one for you to eat now,' said Marjorie. She held it out to Emma.

Sheltie saw the cake and turned his head so far round the other way that the harness creaked. Emma giggled. 'I don't think he'll steal cakes again,' she said.

Once Emma had eaten her cake they trotted back down the lane and past Sally's house at Fox Hall Manor. It would have been nice if Sally had been able to help collect the food, but Sally's mum and dad were having a new floor laid in their big main room and Sally had to stay in and help.

At each house they visited, Emma picked up more boxes of cakes, biscuits and brownies for the party. And each time Sheltie made everyone laugh by refusing to look at the cakes.

Sheltie clopped through the village streets, being careful of the cars. Everyone stopped what they were doing to wave at Emma and Sheltie, and their cart was soon piled high with boxes of goodies for the party.

Mr Grimley and Miss Jenkins were waiting for them outside the wide door that opened the school hall into the playground. 'Perfect timing!' called Mr Grimley, waving the keys. Miss Jenkins took Sheltie by his bridle and ruffled his shaggy mane. Emma jumped out of the cart and loosely tethered Sheltie to the bike stand outside the hall.

As Mr Grimley opened the door, there

was a great rush of water that flowed
down the two steps and lapped over Miss
Jenkins' shoes.

'Oh, my goodness!' cried Miss Jenkins.
'What's happened? Is it a burst pipe or
has someone tried to make a swimming
pool in here?'

Mr Grimley looked shocked. 'What on
earth are we
going to do?'
he asked.

Chapter Four

The hall floor was covered in water.

'It's probably coming from the kitchen,' said Mr Grimley. 'I'll go and see if I can turn it off.'

'There are brushes and buckets in a cupboard near the door over there,' said Emma. 'Perhaps we can brush the water out. I'll go and get them.'

Emma sloshed through the water in her riding boots. It was really very deep – it went right up over her ankles! As she walked, the water rippled like a river under the trestle tables and formed little whirlpools round the legs of the chairs. Emma yanked open a cupboard door and grabbed a couple of big brooms. A plastic bucket that was trying to sail away banged at her legs so she took that too.

Emma filled the bucket and tipped the water outside. Miss Jenkins swept and swept, and a great waterfall fell over the steps into the playground. After ten minutes, everyone's arms ached and the water seemed as deep as ever.

'We'll have to get the fire service to pump it out,' said Mr Grimley. 'The water isn't coming from the kitchen. I don't know where it's all coming from.'

Miss Jenkins swept another waterfall

down the steps, just as Emma's dad arrived in the car with the sandwiches that Mum had made for the party.

'Are you washing the floor?' asked Dad. 'I thought it was pretty clean last night!'

'It's a disaster!' Miss Jenkins told him and showed him the floor inside. 'The hall is flooded. Even if we do get it pumped away, I can't see the hall being ready and dried out before tonight.'

Dad went to the car and put on his wellies. 'I'll help you,' he said.

'But we can't have a party in a wet hall,' said Miss Jenkins. 'We'd better move the plates and cups and tablecloths out, and look for somewhere else. They're in that cupboard next to the little room at the back, aren't they?'

She started to wade through the water, but Sheltie whickered from the doorway and gave Emma an idea.

'Sheltie and I can take all the plates up to the door in one trip,' she said. 'The door's wide enough for the cart.' She went out to untie the little pony from the bicycle stand and unloaded all of the cakes from the little cart into the back of Dad's car.

'We can do it together, Sheltie!' she said, clicking her tongue. 'Up the steps and through to the back!'

The little pony clambered up the steps. Dad lifted the little cart up the steps as they went. Then Sheltie splashed his way through the water to the room at the back of the hall. Miss Jenkins reached into the cupboards and brought out plates and

cups and the big box full of tablecloths.
She handed them down to Emma who
packed them into the cart.

Sheltie was very good as they loaded
the cart, but he was still feeling a bit
frisky after his long rest yesterday. He

nosed at a door nearby, trying to see what was in the little room next to the school kitchen.

'Oh, please be careful, Sheltie!' said Emma. 'Stand still, we're nearly finished.'

She waded through the water to pull his head out of the doorway. And then suddenly she saw where the water was coming from!

Water was spilling into a low sink and splashing down on to a stool next to it. Somebody had left the tap on!

'Sheltie, you're so clever!' cried Emma. 'Did you know that this was where the water was coming from? Look, Dad, the tap's running!'

She leaned over the flooded sink and turned the tap off. Then she took the plug

out of the plughole to let the rest of the
water drain away.

'Well,' said Mr Grimley, 'we won't
need a plumber after all! I wonder who
left that tap on?'

Then Emma remembered that Joshua
was playing in there yesterday. The stool
was just the right height for him to climb
up and reach the tap.

'I bet it was Joshua,' she said. 'He's

been turning taps on all week. It's his new trick.'

She flung her arms round the little pony's neck. 'I should have known you were being clever when you opened that door!' she cried.

Then, with Dad's help, Emma carefully turned Sheltie round. They walked slowly back to the playground again so that Miss Jenkins could take everything out and pack it safely in Dad's car.

The teacher laughed when they told her about Joshua turning on the taps. 'But it isn't funny really,' she said. 'What are we going to do now?'

Nobody in Little Applewood would have enough space for such a big party. Only Fox Hall Manor had a room big enough, but Mr and Mrs Jones were having the new floor put in!

Dad, Miss Jenkins and Mr Grimley put the wet chairs out in the playground to dry in the sun.

'I suppose we'll have to eat our party food in our own houses,' said Mr Grimley. 'It won't be as much fun as a party in the hall.'

Sheltie shook his mane and whickered. He nudged one of the chairs towards the

field with his nose. 'What is that pony up to now?' asked the caretaker.

Sheltie whickered softly at him. Then he nudged at another of the chairs.

Emma giggled. 'Perhaps he wants to play musical chairs!' she said. And then she realized what her pony was doing. 'Sheltie, you're so clever! He wants us to have the party outside!' she said. 'It will be even nicer than having the party in the hall.'

The chairs and trestle tables dried quickly in the sun. In the afternoon, Dad and Mr Grimley rigged up some fairy lights and lanterns in the trees at the edge of the school field, underneath the Little Applewood School banners.

Sheltie came to the party as well, even

though he wasn't invited: Emma had been so excited about the party, she had forgotten to padlock the paddock gate. Sheltie slipped the bolt of his paddock and trotted down the lane to the school field. Everyone was eating and talking very loudly. Suddenly a fuzzy muzzle appeared over Emma's shoulder and knocked over her plate.

'Sheltie! You're not supposed to be here!' said Emma. She jumped out of her seat and ran to catch him as he frisked round the chestnut trees at the edge of the field. He tossed his mane and blew a raspberry at her. Mr Crock took an apple from a basket at the end of their table and went to help Emma.

'I reckon he's the hero of the day,' said Mr Crock. 'And he deserves to be at our party. After all, Sheltie's as much a part of Little Applewood as anyone!'

Sheltie curled his lips in a funny grin. He seemed to agree with everything that Mr Crock said.

The Special Prize

Chapter One

'Will we ever make up our minds?' said Emma. 'There are so many stories to choose from.'

Emma and Sally were sitting on a bench in Minnow's paddock at Fox Hall Manor. Minnow and Sheltie were racing about the field together, but for once their owners weren't watching the ponies. They were searching through piles of books. Most of them were pony stories, but there were lots of others too.

Next Saturday was going to be the last day of Little Applewood School's one hundredth birthday celebrations. There were going to be speeches from former pupils, and the special anniversary plaque would be unveiled in front of everyone. After that there was going to be a grand Barn Dance for all the village in the school hall. But before all this, there was going to be a fancy dress parade. Everyone in the school was going to dress up as a character from a well-known children's book.

Emma had ridden over to Fox Hall Manor to choose a character with Sally. 'We want to do something together,' Emma had told Mrs Jones. 'But it isn't very easy to find two interesting characters who have ponies.'

'I'm sure the two of you will think of something.' Mrs Jones held out a basket of wrinkled apples. 'Oh, by the way, I found these in the apple loft,' she said. 'They're the end of last year's crop and have gone a bit too soft for eating. You can take them for Sheltie and Minnow if you like.'

When Emma and Sally walked over to the fence, Sheltie and Minnow came cantering over, their manes flying. Sheltie leaned his neck over the gate and nuzzled into Emma's hand while Sally palmed Minnow one of the soft apples.

'We could colour in Minnow's white patches and mane. Then he could be Black Beauty,' suggested Emma.

'And if we put some orange dye on Sheltie, he could be Black Beauty's friend, Ginger,' said Sally. They looked at their ponies. They would look great as pony heroes.

Sheltie put his nose over the fence and blew a loud snort, then shook his shaggy mane hard.

'Oh, dear. I don't think Sheltie likes the

idea of having his hair dyed,' said Emma, laughing at the little pony.

'Perhaps he's right,' said Sally. 'Anyway, it might be rather difficult to do. I don't know where we'd get enough hair dye for a whole pony!'

They thought and thought, but they still couldn't come up with anything. At school the next day nobody else had any ideas for how two ponies and two girls could be story characters together. Time was running out. They would have to think of something soon. It looked as though everyone else was having problems finding something different too. There were going to be eight Alice in Wonderlands, four Charlie Buckets, three *Treasure Island* pirates and three witches.

'I'm going to be the best!' boasted

Mark Smith. 'Nobody's thought of who I'm going to be.' Mark was always showing off.

'What's your idea?' asked Emma.

'I'm not telling you,' said Mark. 'It's a secret. My costume's all ready. It's so good, I bet I'll be right at the front of the procession.'

When Emma arrived home she asked Mum to telephone Mrs Jones and ask Sally to tea. 'We've still got to do lots of thinking together,' she said.

'I hope you won't want complicated costumes,' said Mum. 'It's Monday already and I've still got to design a programme for the day.'

Dad frowned and thought. 'Two ponies and two people?' he said. 'That's quite a tall order. How about making it even more difficult by taking Joshua along as well?'

Emma laughed. 'Whatever we think of, we want to be the best in the parade. We've got to be better than Mark Smith. He won't tell anyone what he's doing.'

'He's very sensible to keep it a secret,' said Mum, 'then nobody will be able to copy him. You've already told us that lots of people are doing the same things.'

When Sally arrived at Emma's house on Minnow, they took the black and white pony out to Sheltie's paddock. The two ponies nuzzled at each other then started munching some juicy grass.

Sheltie suddenly began whinnying and flicking his tail. He cantered twice round the paddock and shook out his mane, then charged up to the gate and stopped suddenly with a huge blow. He whickered and pushed his velvety muzzle over the gate. Minnow stopped eating and trotted up to join Sheltie.

'How's my favourite pony?' said a voice. Emma and Sally turned round. It was Mrs Linney, who used to own Sheltie before Emma's family moved into her cottage. Now that she lived in a town flat she couldn't keep a pony, so she was glad that Emma had come along to look after him instead.

Mrs Linney held out a handful of

carrots. Sheltie pushed Minnow aside to get to them first. 'Don't be so greedy, Sheltie!' said Emma. 'Hello, Mrs Linney! I wondered why he was so excited. Have you come for tea too? We need your help.'

Mrs Linney told them that she was staying with Miss Jenkins. Emma and Sally explained about the fancy dress parade, while Mrs Linney gave a handful of carrots to Minnow so that he didn't feel left out. Sheltie turned and stood head to tail against Minnow, swishing his tail happily.

Suddenly Mrs Linney laughed. 'Look at Sheltie! He looks as if he has two heads – one at each end!'

Sally and Emma looked at each other and at the same moment they cried, 'The Pushmi-Pullyu!'

'What are you talking about?' asked
Mrs Linney, looking puzzled.

'In *Doctor Dolittle*,' said Emma
breathlessly. 'It's the strange animal that
the Doctor brought back from his travels.'

'It had a head at both ends,' explained
Sally. 'It's the perfect idea for a costume.'

Mrs Linney laughed. 'How are you
going to persuade Minnow and Sheltie to
walk head to tail like that in the parade?
One of them would have to walk
backwards all the time. I know Sheltie is

106

a very clever pony, and *sometimes* behaves very well, but do you really think he could do that?'

Emma giggled. 'We could put an extra head on the other end of him,' she explained. 'Perhaps we could make it out of cardboard or papier mâché.'

'And what about Minnow?' asked Mrs Linney. 'I thought you wanted them to be together?'

Sally thought hard. 'Doctor Dolittle had lots of animals,' she said. 'Minnow can be a zebra. He's black and white already but we could paint a sheet to put over him and make him striped.'

Sheltie threw his head back and gave a loud whinny.

'There you are,' said Mrs Linney. 'It sounds as if Sheltie approves!'

Chapter Two

'It's a good idea,' said Mum. She cut
some sponge cake into fingers for little
Joshua and handed him a piece. 'But
where are you going to get an extra head
from, Emma? And if you tie something to
Sheltie's tail end, he'll probably try to get
rid of it.'

'I think I have the very thing,' said Mrs
Linney. 'I've got a Western saddle that
my husband once brought back from

America. There's a little back rest at the end. It's like riding in an armchair. It's far too big for Sheltie, of course, but so long as you didn't ride him in the parade we could use it to fix another head on to the back rest bit.'

Emma and Sally grinned. That sounded like the perfect answer!

'Who's going to be the Doctor?' asked Dad. He looked at Emma and then at Sally. 'The Doctor was quite a plump chap, as far as I remember. We'll have to choose the fattest of you.'

Emma and Sally looked at each other and giggled.

'Emma!' said Joshua. He beamed and waved his cake at her.

'Emma it is, then,' said Dad. 'I've got some old clothes you can wear, and we'll

fill out a jumper with hay for his big
tummy.'

'But what about Sally?' said Mrs
Linney.

'Polynesia the parrot was the Doctor's
best friend, wasn't she?' said Mum.
'Perhaps Sally could be a parrot.'

'Parrot!' echoed Joshua, clapping his
hands with the sponge cake still in them.

'I think I might be too big for a parrot,'
said Sally. 'But his other best friend was

Chee-Chee the monkey. I'd like to be a monkey!'

'I haven't got time to make a monkey costume!' said Mum, alarmed. 'I haven't even started on my programmes!'

'I'll ask my mum if she'll make the costumes,' said Sally. 'She's very good at sewing.'

'Parrot!' said Joshua again. He really liked that word.

Emma looked at him in his bright red jumper and his bright green trousers. They were perfect parrot colours.

'And Joshua can be Polynesia the parrot!' cried Emma.

'That sounds a splendid idea, Emma,' said Mrs Linney. 'And I've had another idea. When I was a little girl I had a hobby-horse. It was a horse's head on a

long stick with a wheel at the other end.
You sat on the stick and held the bridle,
just like a real horse. What you want is an
old hobby-horse head. I wonder if
anyone has one that they would lend
you.'

Emma jumped up. 'We'll visit everyone
after school tomorrow and ask. Somebody
must have one!'

After school on Tuesday, Emma and Sally
took Sheltie and Minnow to visit all their
friends and ask if anyone had an old
hobby-horse head that they could borrow.
But although they visited everyone they
could think of, nobody had one.

'Who was that?' said Sally as they
came away from Mrs Marsh's house. 'I
thought I saw someone spying on us!'

Emma turned her head quickly. She just caught a quick movement behind Mrs Marsh's garden shed. 'Maybe it was a cat,' she said.

'Funny,' said Sally. 'It looked more like a small person to me. And Mrs Marsh hasn't got any children.'

By the time they reached the bridle path leading to Beacon Hill, Sheltie and Minnow were tired of walking quietly from house to house. Sheltie was tugging at his reins and becoming quite restless. He wanted to race along.

'One more stop, Sheltie,' said Emma, 'but you can have a good gallop on the way. We're going to Marjorie Wallace's cottage.' The girls tightened their reins and squeezed their legs. Sheltie and

Minnow raced each other over the fields until the girls had to pull on the reins to slow them down.

Emma dismounted quickly outside Marjorie's cottage and knocked on the red front door. Sally climbed down from Minnow and took Sheltie's reins in her hands.

'Hello, Emma,' said Marjorie. 'I was just going to telephone you. I've been having a clear-out. I wondered if you and Sheltie could carry these things down to the village hall in the fish cart some time. The cricket club is having a jumble sale soon. Come and have some juice and biscuits, and I'll show you what's there.'

'Of course we'll take them,' said Emma. 'We'll bring the cart up tomorrow.'

Over orange juice and biscuits, Sally and Emma explained about their Doctor Dolittle theme and the Pushmi-Pullyu.

'But if we can't find a horse's head to put on Sheltie, we'll have to try and make one,' said Emma.

Marjorie began to laugh. 'What a good thing I waited for you to take my jumble to the sale,' she said. 'You're only just in time. Look what I was going to throw out!'

She moved the big sofa at the back of the room. Behind it, at the top of a heap of jumble, was an old rocking horse with its head half falling off!

Chapter Three

The next evening, Dad helped Emma to strap the fish cart's harness on to Sheltie. Sally said she'd ride Minnow to Marjorie's cottage too, to help load up the cart.

When they arrived at the cottage, Marjorie was waiting for them.

'I hope Sheltie's not going to mind,' Emma said to Marjorie, as she took the rocking-horse head from her. 'Mrs Linney is going to try the Western saddle and let him get used to that first. The rocking-horse head will look great – much better than a cardboard one.'

'I'm glad it will come in useful,' said Marjorie.

When everything was loaded up, they waved goodbye to Marjorie. They made their way home along the bridle path by Bramble Woods because the ground was more level and they didn't want to upset the cart.

Just as they came out of the winding bridle path into the lane, the cart seemed to rock and Emma almost fell out.

Sally came up on Minnow. 'Are you all right?' she asked anxiously. 'What's wrong with Sheltie?'

'It's all right,' said Emma. She made

little soothing noises to calm Sheltie down. 'It wasn't Sheltie's fault. I thought I saw someone in the bushes and it made me jump. I must have jerked the reins.'

'I didn't see anyone,' said Sally. 'Perhaps it was a dog.'

Emma didn't think it was a dog. It had looked more like a person. But if it was a person, why were they hiding?

When they got home, they unpacked the cart and Dad looked at the rocking horse with the wobbly head. It was so wobbly that when he gave it a tug, it came away from the wooden body.

'There won't be any problem fixing that on to the Western saddle,' he said. 'But I think we'd better leave it in Sheltie's field shelter so that he gets friendly with his other head!'

Sheltie wasn't too sure about the
rocking-horse head. He blew and
whickered as Dad carried it across the
paddock, then he turned and trotted over
to his field shelter to look at it more
closely. Emma ran across too. Sheltie
looked down and shook his head at the
wooden horse's mane. He pawed it with

his front hoof and then, as if he was satisfied that it wasn't real, he settled down beside it.

Emma wanted to giggle. Sheltie looked so funny lying down beside a wooden horse's head . . .

As they came out of the shelter, Emma thought she saw someone dart towards the hedge at the bottom of the paddock, but it was beginning to get dark and it was hard to see properly. 'I wonder who that is,' she said. Emma had the feeling that someone was spying on her.

Dad had seen something move too. 'Probably a fox,' he said.

But Emma was sure it was a person. A person about the same size as her and Sally. Tomorrow she'd go and investigate to see what someone might find so

interesting at the end of Sheltie's
paddock.

When Emma came home from school the
next day, Sheltie met her at the paddock
gate and pushed his soft muzzle into her
hands, hoping for a juicy, sweet apple.

Emma gave him a big hug. 'You're
going to have the best costume in the
parade, Sheltie! Dad says he'll try to fix
your new head on the saddle tonight.
Come on, let's go and get it.'

Emma tried to move towards the
shelter, but Sheltie barged against her,
pushing his face into hers. 'What's
wrong?' Emma asked, grabbing his head
collar and pushing him away. 'Don't be
silly, Sheltie. I'm only going to take it to
Dad to put it on the Western saddle.'

But when Emma reached the shelter, the rocking-horse head was not there. She stared at the little pony, who stood there tossing his mane as if to say, I was trying to tell you, but you wouldn't listen.

'What have you done with it, Sheltie?' asked Emma.

Sheltie blew a long whicker and pushed against her again, nosing into her back and butting her so that she had to move towards the far corner of his paddock. 'Have you hidden it there, Sheltie? All right, I'll get it and take it away.'

Emma felt sad. Maybe Sheltie didn't want to be dressed up as a Pushmi-Pullyu after all.

The paddock sloped down a little in the far corner. It would be just the place for Sheltie to hide something, thought Emma. She looked around, staring into the hedge. But Sheltie shoved at her impatiently, whickered softly and nudged her to a particular part of the hedge. 'Is this where you've put it?' asked Emma. Then she noticed something.

There was a long horse hair hanging from the hedge, about the length of a pony's mane. But it wasn't the same

colour as Sheltie's mane or even
Minnow's. It was the same colour as the
rocking horse's mane.

Emma remembered how Sheltie had
settled down beside the rocking-horse
head the night before. Of course he
wasn't afraid of it! Then she remembered
something else. There had been someone
watching them yesterday. Had that
someone taken the rocking-horse head
away?

'Can you help me find the thief,
Sheltie?' said Emma. Sheltie lifted his
head and snorted.

Chapter Four

Quickly, Emma ran for Sheltie's saddle
and bridle. Then she rode him out of the
paddock and round to the other side of
the hedge where they had found the wisp
of horse mane.

The hedge was a bit broken at the
bottom, as if someone big had pushed
through the tangled branches. Or as if
someone small holding a rocking-horse
head had pushed through.

Emma held the reins loosely in her hands and let Sheltie go his own way. He trotted past Mr Crock's cottage, then clattered over the little stone bridge at the end of the lane that led to the village. In the village, his hoofs went *clip clop* on the hard road. Mrs Marsh waved as she came out of the baker's shop, but Sheltie didn't stop to say hello. He seemed to be making for the end of the village.

Then Sheltie suddenly stopped. Coming out of the post office was Mark Smith with a large lollipop in his hand.

Sheltie trotted over to Mark and stretched out his neck.

'Help! Get your horrible pony off me!' Mark cried. He hid the lollipop behind his back.

'Don't be scared,' said Emma. She slid

off Sheltie's back and led the little
Shetland pony closer to Mark. 'Just give
him a pat, he likes that.'

'He'll eat my lollipop!' shouted Mark.

'He doesn't like them at the moment,'
said Emma. 'He got sick eating too much
sweet stuff. Don't worry.'

And then she saw a horse hair wound
round one of Mark's coat buttons. It was
the same colour as the hair in the hedge,
and the same colour as the rocking-horse
mane. Now Emma understood why
Sheltie had
stopped.

'Where have you put our rocking-horse head?' she cried suddenly.

'I – I don't know what you mean!' said Mark, stumbling over his words. 'I don't know anything about your old rocking-horse head. I hate horses!'

Sheltie gave a rude snort, which made Mark step back even further.

At that moment, Mrs Smith, Mark's mum, came out of the post office.

'What's this about a rocking-horse head?' she said. 'Mark brought one home yesterday, Emma. He said nobody wanted it. Is it yours?'

Emma explained about the Pushmi-Pullyu and the rocking-horse head. Mrs Smith looked at her son very severely.

'You told me someone gave it to you for *your* costume!' she said to Mark.

'It was in an old shed,' Mark said. 'I didn't think anyone wanted it.'

'It wasn't in a shed,' said Emma. 'It was in Sheltie's field shelter. And anyway,' she added, 'if you didn't think anyone wanted it, why didn't you ask for it?'

And then Emma suddenly remembered all the times she thought she had seen someone spying on her and Sally. 'You *knew* we wanted it for the parade,' she exclaimed. 'You stole it!'

Mark looked scared. 'I didn't steal it!' he said. 'I was only going to hide it for a while. I thought your costume might be better than my King Arthur one, and I wanted to stop you.'

'You've been very naughty, Mark,' said Mrs Smith. 'You don't deserve to be in the parade at all. King Arthur was a good king. How can you pretend to be a good king like Arthur if you go around stealing things?'

But Emma could see that Mark was really sorry. He was looking at Sheltie and holding his hand out nervously to try and make friends. Mark wasn't so bad really. He just showed off a lot.

'I'm really sorry, Emma,' he said. 'It was a stupid thing to do. I bet your costume will be really good.'

Emma nodded. 'So will yours,' she said.

Emma and Sheltie went to collect the rocking-horse head and with Mark and Mrs Smith's help, they managed to fix it to Mrs Linney's Western saddle. Sheltie didn't make any fuss at all, but when the saddle was on his back, he turned around and whinnied to the new head.

'Look!' laughed Emma. 'He's trying to make friends with it.'

Dad left the saddle and the head in Sheltie's field shelter so that he could get used to both of them over the next two nights.

Now all that was left to sort out were the costumes. Mrs Jones had finished Sally's Chee-Chee costume. It was made of a soft fawn fluffy material and had a long tail with a curl at the end. And for a surprise she had made a special parrot jacket for little Joshua to wear over his red jumper and green trousers. There was a little hood with a parrot beak on it and his arms went into short wings.

Joshua wasn't quite sure about his costume. His head darted round and round, looking for Mum. 'Oh, Joshua, you look exactly like a little parrot when you do that!' said Emma. She ran to give him a big hug.

Joshua beamed. 'Parrot!' he said.

Saturday came at last. Dad put his old jumper over Emma's head and stuffed hay into it to make a fat tummy. Emma giggled. The hay was tickly. She put Dad's old jacket on over the top and did up the buttons. 'Go on, both of you,' said Dad. 'See what Sheltie thinks of you.'

Emma took Joshua in his parrot costume to show Sheltie. The little pony galloped across to the gate to meet them. He seemed to know this was a special day. Sheltie rolled over on to his back, kicking up his heels, then did a little dance in front of everyone. Joshua laughed and waved his arms about, so that he really did look like a flying parrot!

Sheltie put his head over the gate and nuzzled at Emma. His pony mouth pushed its way into Emma's jumper and began to pull at it.

'No, Sheltie! You mustn't eat my stuffing!' giggled Emma. But he managed to nibble a mouthful of hay as well as a corner of Dad's old jumper before Emma found a couple of carrots in her pocket for him to eat instead.

After lunch, Dad and Mrs Linney fixed the Western saddle with its rocking-horse head on to Sheltie's back. He stood very still and seemed to know that he had to behave from now on.

Emma was rather nervous when Sally

rode over on Minnow in his zebra stripes. She was worried that Sheltie might confuse or frighten the other pony. Sheltie nodded his head at the sight of his friend, but he still didn't move.

Then Minnow walked round to Sheltie's hindquarters and pushed his face against the rocking-horse head. He seemed rather puzzled that the head didn't nuzzle him back! 'Poor Minnow!' said Emma. 'He doesn't know which end to talk to!'

*

When they arrived at the school, Mr Price, the headmaster, was organizing everybody in the parade. He looked at Sheltie. 'I don't know whether to put you at the beginning or the end of the procession!' he joked. But in the end everyone wanted Doctor Dolittle to go in front, leading his friends, Chee-Chee the monkey, Zig Zag the zebra, and his special friend the Pushmi-Pullyu, with Polynesia the parrot sitting on his back.

There was a special prize for the best costume and the judges were so impressed by Sheltie's back-to-front heads and Minnow's zebra stripes that they gave Emma and Sally the first prize.

Proudly, Emma and Sally led their ponies up to the judge's table. But now that the parade was over, Sheltie didn't

have to behave properly any more. He
snatched the list of winners from the table
and dashed away with it.

'Sheltie, come back!' scolded Emma, but
everyone else could hardly stop laughing.
Sheltie looked so funny with his extra
head bumping about on Mrs Linney's
Western saddle!

Sheltie did behave himself later that day
though. When Mr Price unveiled the

special plaque in front of all the villagers and lots of former pupils in the school hall, Sheltie stood quietly in the wide doorway with Emma.

'I've said thank you to a lot of people for their help in making Little Applewood's one hundredth birthday so special,' said Mr Price. 'But there's one person – or rather one pony – who deserves a special thank you. What would we have done without him? A round of applause, please, for Sheltie!'

Everybody clapped madly and then laughed when Sheltie answered with the loudest raspberry he had ever blown in his life!

If you like making friends, fun, excitement and adventure, then you'll love

The little pony with the big heart!

Sheltie is the lovable little Shetland pony with a big personality. He is cheeky, full of fun and has a heart of gold. His owner, Emma, knew that she and Sheltie would be best friends as soon as she saw him. She could tell that he thought so too by the way his brown eyes twinkled beneath his big, bushy mane. When Emma, her mum and dad and little brother, Joshua, first moved to Little Applewood, she thought that she might not like living there. But life is never dull with Sheltie around. He is full of mischief and he and Emma have lots of exciting adventures together.

Share Sheltie and Emma's adventures in:

SHELTIE THE SHETLAND PONY
SHELTIE SAVES THE DAY
SHELTIE AND THE RUNAWAY
SHELTIE FINDS A FRIEND
SHELTIE TO THE RESCUE
SHELTIE IN DANGER